Max Brinkley's Military BRAT Mysteries

THE CASE OF THE
DING-DONG DITCHER

Max Brinkley's Military BRAT Mysteries

THE CASE OF THE DING-DONG DITCHER

By Kim Roedl
Illustrations by Mindy J.B. Whitten

BELLE ISLE BOOKS
www.belleislebooks.com

Printed in the United States

ISBN: 978-1-9399307-1-2
Library of Congress Control Number: 2016942641

Published by Belle Isle Books

BELLE ISLE BOOKS
www.belleislebooks.com

This book is dedicated to all military children—past, present, and future. I stand in awe of your strength. Thank you to my five military brats. A special mention also to Jackson, Bryce, and Heidi Hallett, whose father made the ultimate sacrifice in Afghanistan in 2009.

CHAPTER 1
THE NEW KID (AGAIN)

Max Brinkley sat at the kitchen table, staring glumly at the fork he was using to move his cheesy scrambled eggs from one side of the plate to the other.

"I think that asking a kid to go through TWO first days of school in one year is cruel and unusual punishment," Max said, rolling his eyes. "This kinda thing has to be illegal in most states."

His little brother, Knox, laughed out loud, sending bits of his mouthful of cereal and milk dribbling down his green long-sleeved shirt. Max grimaced and scooted his chair away from him.

"Oh, that was SMOOTH," he scoffed. Knox, unaware that he was annoying his brother, continued his attempt to comfort Max.

"I'm pretty sure there's no *actual* law that prevents it. I could probably help you write a letter to our congressman when we get home from school today, though," Knox said matter-of-factly.

Max usually didn't get annoyed when his totally genius seven-year-old brother chimed in with a solution to his problems. This morning was different, though. This was no time to have a younger brother with an IQ of 159.

"Can you just be normal for once?" Max asked as he slammed his elbows on the table. "There's got to be normal seven-year-old stuff floating around in that genius brain of yours."

Knox slumped in his chair, looking more like a scolded puppy than an elementary-school super genius. Actually, Knox *looked* totally normal. He had sandy brown hair, tapered on the sides but long and spiky on top, so he could use plenty of hair gel; large green eyes; and tiny freckles alongside his nose. He was pretty stylish for his age. Secretly reading his mom's fashion magazines was his guilty pleasure. People couldn't tell just by looking at Knox that his mind was moving a mile a minute. They *could* always tell that Knox and Max were brothers. Max was like a taller, darker-haired version of Knox, with curly hair and large, light brown eyes. Max liked to think he was better-looking, though.

The family had only been in Sumter, South Carolina, for a week. They'd settled in a quiet, wooded neighborhood about fifteen minutes from the military installation where Max's father was now stationed. Everyone (except for Max, of course) was excited about this new adventure. Max's mom, a former professional photographer, talked non-stop about having the chance to take photographs of the aging farmhouses and abandoned wooden shacks she'd seen dotting the winding, rural fields throughout the county. His dad said being stationed only a couple hours from historic Charleston, the beaches, and Savannah would give the family lots to do during vacation time. Knox was excited because he wanted to visit the science museum in Columbia.

Whoop-dee-doo, thought Max. He missed "his" small town—DuPont—in Washington State so much. There was nothing like hiking to the Puget Sound on a day that wasn't so rainy, or whale-watching on San Juan Island with his best friend, Matt Jacobs. He had grown to love watching storms roll in, and playing in the rain with no raincoat. Life was so good then. Max wasn't sure he wanted to give living in South Carolina a chance.

He had been happy, though, to see the moving truck finally arrive with all of the family's household goods. He'd been so upset about moving that he had mistakenly packed up all his electronic devices and let the movers take them. His mom told him it was a good excuse to read books during the week-long car trip from Washington State to South Carolina. The day before they departed, she'd handed him a stack of old mystery books. The dust jackets were faded and torn. One looked like a mouse had chewed on it.

"I didn't send these with the movers because I was planning on donating them," she explained. "I used to love these books as a kid."

Max had taken one look at the covers and scowled. "Mom! These books have to be like a *hundred* years old!"

His mother gave him a look that said she wasn't amused. "Suit yourself, Maxwell, but it's going to be a long trip, and I don't want to hear any fussing. And besides, there's nothing like a good, old-fashioned mystery."

Two hours into the drive, Max gave in and opened the first book. And though he would *never* admit it to his mom, it was actually pretty good! Soon he was caught up trying to solve the mysteries for himself. By the time the Brinkleys' SUV crossed the South Carolina state line, Max had finished the entire stack.

But now those books were stashed away in a corner of his new room, and Max forced his thoughts to return to the school day ahead. He didn't want to think about Washington right now. Remembering everything he'd left behind just made him feel worse. Today all Max could think of was the fact that in the next hour, he was going to start sixth grade all over again—in the middle of the year, with new teachers and kids he didn't know.

"Knox, if you were really so smart, you would have known I wasn't being serious. I know there's no law like that. Geesh," Max said. "I wish there *was* a law that made it illegal to move without having your kids' permission."

He flopped his head onto the breakfast table. His mom, who was feeding his twin baby sisters a bowl of oatmeal while unpacking boxes of kitchen supplies, leaned over and kissed the top of his head. Their dad, who has been silently eating his breakfast, stared sympathetically at Max.

"I know this is hard for you, big guy, but that's not a good reason for you to be mean to your brother. He's starting at a new school today too, and he's trying his best to make you feel better," Dad said. He stood up, grabbed his uniform jacket from the back of his chair, and put it on. "Max, moving every two or three years isn't easy for any of us. It's even harder when we can't be together during deployments. At least we're together right now, right?"

Max knew he couldn't argue with that. It had been almost a year ago that his dad returned from a yearlong deployment to Afghanistan, and he had missed so much—Max's baseball games, Knox's big win at the state science fair, and the birth of Max's twin sisters, Heidi and Harley. Dad had told them all how much he'd thought of them every day while he was away.

Dad's time in Afghanistan was spent working long hours; staring at a computer screen in a windowless office made of plywood, or involved in missions to secure cities and villages. Max never told anyone that he worried his dad would be injured or even killed during his deployment.

Sometimes he and Knox cried because they missed their dad so much. His mom would always hold them and say everything would be all right. Max remembered watching his mom's face when they saw their dad for the first time after redeployment. It was the first time he'd ever seen her cry. Mom had insisted those were tears of joy.

This PCS (Permanent Change of Station) meant that his dad might have to deploy again, but Max didn't want to think about that now. They were together in this new place, and Max was thankful.

Max looked at his dad.

"I know you're right, Dad. Everything will be fine today. It's just that I was finally becoming one of the cool kids at my old school."

Dad smiled. "I'm sure you'll be just as cool or maybe even cooler at Carolina Jasmine Elementary/Middle School," he said. Knox gave Max a high five.

"Yes, I think there is a high probability of you being one of the most awesome dudes at CJEMS," Knox said.

"You wouldn't understand, Knox. I'm in middle school. I'm not a little kid anymore. Life is more complicated," Max sighed. "There are lots of things to consider—my hair, girls, my almost-mustache…"

Dad handed Max and Knox their backpacks, then put on his patrol cap.

"Knox is right. You'll both fit right in. Max, your hair looks great, and well, the girl thing will one day work itself out." He opened the door. "Come on, guys, I'll walk you to school."

Mom, holding a hand of each of the twins, followed them to the front door. "You know, Max, if you really don't want to start school today, you can always stay home with me and unpack some boxes."

Max stepped out of the house.

"While I would LOVE to unpack boxes with you, Mom, I think I'd better get this show on the road," he laughed. "Middle school waits for no one!"

Max breathed in the fresh, crisp February air. He stood there for a second, watching the dozens of children walk down the sidewalk toward the school. He was ready. What was he worried about anyway? By now, he was an old pro at moving. He had done it three times before.

When Max was born, his family had been stationed at Fort Bliss in El Paso, Texas, and they lived there until he was three. Thinking of El Paso always brought back fuzzy memories of watching dust devils tear through the streets. Max had been too young to remember much about the year his father went on an unaccompanied tour to Korea. But he couldn't forget moving into a rental house in his grandparents' neighborhood in Alabama. Grandpa Jonas had taken him to the zoo once a week.

That was also the year Knox was born. Max thought it was pretty cool to be a big brother, especially to someone too young to play with Max's toys. After their dad returned home, the family PCSed to Fort Riley, Kansas. Max was intrigued by the howling Kansas winds, the hotter-than-hot summers, and the turn-into-a-human-popsicle winters.

When Max was seven, his dad received orders to Joint Base Lewis-McChord in Washington State. Then, just as the Pacific Northwest was beginning to feel like home, it was time to move again. Now they were more than 2,000 miles away, in South Carolina.

His dad had always told him to think about the moves as new adventures. This was just a new adventure. Max decided to buck up and look at it that way.

"I guess a second first day of school isn't so bad," he announced to his family with a grin. "Watch out, Carolina Jasmine Elementary/Middle, Max Brinkley is definitely in the HOUSE!"

Unable to control himself, he broke into his famous victory dance. The twins, watching from the porch, mimicked their big brother, clumsily knocking their little knees together and attempting to shake their hips.

Knox laughed and began to run down the sidewalk.

"Race ya!" Knox screamed. Max took off after his brother.

CHAPTER 2

SPELLING BEE. WHO, ME?

Max was relieved to find out he wasn't the only new kid in Mrs. Rice's sixth-grade homeroom. Three new kids had arrived in the last month. He and a curly-haired girl named Charlotte Rochester were both joining the English class that same day.

Charlotte seemed to be very shy. She talked softly and stared at the floor a lot. Mrs. Rice told each of them to choose an empty desk. Max looked around the room and spotted one next to a girl with long dark hair and freckles on her nose. Max couldn't help smiling. The girl was definitely really cute. She had her glossy hair pulled behind her ears, revealing two small pearl earrings. Her khaki pants were neatly ironed, and she wore a crisp white shirt under her soft pink sweater. When Max sat down, the cute girl smiled back at him.

She leaned over and whispered, "I'm Celia Honeywell. Nice to meet you." Max could feel his face getting hot. He hoped she didn't know he was blushing.

"I'm Max. G-glad to meet you," he managed to stutter. He couldn't say what he was really thinking: "A face without freckles is like the night sky without stars." Max smiled to himself as Mrs. Rice tapped her yardstick on her desk to get everyone's attention.

"Okay, boys and girls, as most of you know, it's time for our class spelling bee. The winner will advance to the school spelling bee. The runner-up will serve as an alternate. Everyone stand up beside your desk," Mrs. Rice said.

Max looked around and slowly stood up. He was excited. Spelling was his favorite subject. Mrs. Rice looked at him.

"Max, since you and Charlotte haven't had a chance to study the words, you are not required to participate," she said.

Charlotte sat down. Max wasn't going to sit

down. He was determined to show off his extreme coolness to Celia, his new crush.

"If you don't mind, Mrs. Rice, I would like to be in the spelling bee," he said. Mrs. Rice nodded her approval.

Once the bee got underway, it didn't take long for most of the other students to be eliminated. Max was chuckling to himself. *I've got this win in the bag*, he thought.

Max was caught up in the excitement of the competition. He nervously bit his lip and rocked on his heels. "Anxious," "calendar," "squirrel"— Max rattled them all off flawlessly. A short girl with blond hair spelled "example" incorrectly, and there were suddenly only two contestants left.

Oh no! thought Max, looking around the room. Celia, beautiful Celia, was his opponent! Her arms were folded, and she didn't look too happy. In fact, she looked more like a bull that wanted to charge him. It might only be his imagination, but he swore he could hear growling coming from her direction. Still, pretty girl or no pretty girl, Max was in the zone, and he wasn't about to throw the match.

Beating her was proving to be a challenge, though. They continued to go head-to-head. Max was sure Celia would not be able to spell "acoustics." Celia seemed disappointed when Max spelled "xylophone." With every correct word Max uttered, Celia stomped her foot. Mrs. Rice reminded her about good sportsmanship. Max started to relax, feeling certain that this spelling bee was his to win. It was his turn. His word? *Mistletoe.* Max gave a devilish smile. Ha! There was no way he could get this word wrong. With confidence, he spelled the word: m-i-s-s-l-e-t-o-e. When Celia giggled, he knew his battleship was sunk.

"That is incorrect, Max. If Celia can spell the word correctly, she wins," Mrs. Rice said.

Celia cleared her throat and then spoke: "M-i-s-*t*-l-e-t-o-e."

Mrs. Rice nodded and announced Celia the class winner. Max lowered his head. He'd lost to the cute girl. He would not let on to her that he was disappointed, though. He was a good sport.

The other boys in the class gathered around to congratulate him.

"Good going, Max! You are the MAN," said Hector Martinez.

"You sure are," echoed Benjamin Richards. "There aren't many people who can go head-to-head with Celia."

Max beamed with pride. "It was nothing, you guys," he said with a smile.

The bell rang. Celia tapped him on the shoulder. *Be cool*, Max thought. He turned toward her, grinning from ear to ear, ready to shake the victor's hand. Instead, Celia stood there with her arms crossed.

"What was all of that back there?" she asked. Max was confused.

"I don't know what you mean," he stammered. Celia glared at him.

"Since you're new, I'll give you the benefit of the doubt this time. Obviously you don't know any better." Celia grinned now, but it wasn't a nice grin. She tucked a stray hair behind her ear, then stepped close to Max.

"Let's get something straight. I am the smartest kid in this class, and don't you forget it," she whispered in his ear. "You got lucky today. That's all it was. You won't be so lucky next time, and I won't be so nice."

And with that, she walked away, leaving a stunned Max Brinkley in her wake.

Max's crush on Celia Honeywell was crushed. No amount of nastiness could erase the fact that Celia was the prettiest girl he had ever seen, but something deep down in his gut was telling him to stay far, far away from her. Still, it was hard not to stand there watching Celia fling her beautiful hair from her absolutely perfect, freckly face as she glided toward the door.

Hector's voice broke his trance.

"Hey, Max! It's time for second period! We can't be late to math."

"Yeah, okay!"

Max let out a sigh. He'd have to make sure to write down the first lesson he'd learned on his second first day of school: Watch out for pretty girls who can spell. Noted! Max ran to catch up with his new friends.

CHAPTER 3
SMART COOKIES

Max had plenty to share about his school day at dinner that night. He bragged to his family that his friend Hector could turn his eyelids inside out. He was super excited that the cafeteria served cheese pizza every Friday. He even told his parents about the class spelling bee. His mom was proud that he had tried his best. His dad was sure that Max would never forget how to spell 'mistletoe.'

Max agreed. While he "forgot on purpose" to tell everyone about his run-in with Celia, there was something he could not *wait* to tell them.

"My science teacher *does not* blink," he said with a straight face. "Seriously!"

Knox, who had been busy counting the peas on his plate, turned his attention to his brother. "Impossible. Everyone blinks. In fact, the average person blinks at least fifteen times a minute," Knox said.

"Well, from where I was sitting, he didn't look like he blinked once. I'll have to pay more attention tomorrow," Max replied.

"Of course the blink rate for each human varies…" Knox continued.

"Very cool," Max said with a smile. "We should test it. Watch my eyes." He tried his hardest not to blink as he stared down his brother.

"You blinked," Knox said matter-of-factly.

Their mother looked at her sons with interest. "Knox, how was your first day?"

Knox paused before answering.

"We got to climb a rock wall in PE today. I made it all the way to the top, and rang the bell. That was pretty awesome," he proudly announced.

"That does sound like fun," Mom said. "Did you like your new class?" Knox nodded.

"Well, the class is learning how to solve inequalities. Since I've been doing that for a couple of years now, Mrs. Holt said I could help her out by being a tutor, so I won't get bored," he said.

Knox had started doing basic math and reading on a sixth-grade level by the time he was five years old. A year later, he'd been offered membership into Mensa, a high-IQ society for kids and adults. Educators had been urging the Brinkleys to put Knox into middle school so he could at least be academically challenged, but his parents would only agree to let him skip one grade. Knox liked third grade and was allowed to take extra-elevated online coursework when he wanted. Even though he was really smart, he was still a curious little boy who loved playing video games, building models, and breakdancing. He also looked up to Max and took every opportunity to tag behind his brother. To Knox, eleven-year-old Max was one of the smartest guys in the world. It didn't even matter that Max had trouble with long division and had no idea what the difference between erosion and weathering was.

"Sounds like both of you guys had a great day. Your mom and I are so glad. Anyone want to hear about my day? I got a chance to go to my new office today and meet some of the soldiers I'll be working with…" Dad was interrupted by the doorbell ringing.

"Who could that be?" Dad asked. He got up from the dinner table and headed for the front door.

"Maybe one of the neighbors is bringing us a plate of cookies for dessert. That would be AMAZING," Max said, jumping up to join his father.

Dad opened the door. No one was there. Max stuck his head out and peered into the darkness. He didn't see anyone—only a dark cat scurrying into a bush.

Dad shrugged his shoulders and closed the door. They headed back for the dining room.

"Hmm. No one was there. Maybe they had the wrong house," Dad said.

"Great, that means that someone else is getting our cookies," Max joked.

"Since everyone had such a wonderful day, I think we all deserve some cookies. I'll bake some," Mom said. Both boys shouted their approval and went into the kitchen to help.

CHAPTER 4

THE TALL KID WHO DOESN'T FIT IN

It had only been a couple of weeks, but Max had already decided he really liked his new school. His teachers were all pretty cool, even though he was convinced that Mr. Collins never blinked. He had lots of new friends who laughed at his jokes, always saved a seat for him at lunch, and walked home with him after school. Life was good again for Max Brinkley.

On Friday, after lunch, Max ran to grab the tire swing before any of his friends could claim it. It was break time, and their teachers let them wander over to the elementary school playground. The other boys soon joined him, choosing to scamper on either side of the huge outdoor jungle gym. Max was enjoying goofing off with his friends—until he spotted another boy who was sitting alone in the shade of the school building. Max recognized the tall, lanky boy as one of his classmates.

"Guys, let's ask him if he wants to play. If we had another person, we could TOTALLY play dodgeball," Max said. Hector, who was dangling from the monkey bars, jumped down and ran over to his friend.

"Max, are you looking for trouble? That kid is all sorts of loco!" Hector said.

Max was puzzled. "What are you talking about? He's just a kid like us," he said.

"Hector's right," chimed in Mark Lawrence, adjusting his glasses as he stared down from the top of the jungle gym. "I heard that guy is really supposed to be in eighth grade. Look at him! He's taller than anyone else in sixth grade."

Max looked again. The boy *was* pretty tall, with skinny arms and legs and a mop of wavy black hair that was constantly falling into his face. But he didn't look like an eighth-grader to Max. And he certainly didn't look like a crazy person.

By now, other kids had grown interested in the conversation and made their way over. "His name is Finn Harper," Jonathan Parker volunteered. Finn was new in town, too, and had started school a few weeks before Max.

"I heard he stole a car, drove it all the way to Canada, and pretended to be a grown-up for six whole months before his parents tracked him down!"

Max couldn't believe what he was hearing. "You guys, do you really think any of that could be true? He doesn't look like a grown-up. Grown-ups have full mustaches and beards and stuff. I really think we need to give him a chance. There is no way—"

Hector didn't let Max finish.

"You can take your chances with him if you want, but you'll have to do that on your own. Right you guys?" Hector looked around for support. The other kids nodded. "So you're either his friend, or our friend."

Max felt terrible, because he knew he had no choice. He didn't want to be an outsider. He didn't want people saying he was a juvenile delinquent who had robbed a bank before moving to town. Max just wanted to be normal and one of the guys. He sighed.

"Of course you guys are my friends," he said. "I just thought…"

Before he could finish, the bell rang, signaling the end of break. The class ran from the playground. Far off, Finn stood and slowly headed for the line that was forming by the school door.

Max watched him trudging all alone, shoulders slumped as if he wanted to look shorter, or maybe even disappear altogether. Common sense told Max there was no way Finn was guilty of any of those things the other kids said he'd done. But how in the world could Max prove it without everyone turning on him? He couldn't prove anything, and he didn't want to risk his place within his new friend group. Poor Finn! And poor Max.

CHAPTER 5

DING-DONG, WHO WAS IT?

Max loved the weekends, but not for the obvious reasons. Sure, school was out, but the added bonus was that in the Brinkley household, weekends were reserved for family time. It had been that way for as long as he could remember. Time together was precious, because the family never knew when Dad would be away on a training exercise or work trip or another deployment. Day trips were common, especially when they had lived in the Seattle area. Max loved wandering around Pike Place Market. People-watching was his thing. He especially liked to watch the guys throw around the fish in the market. One time he got picked to catch one of the fish. That went down on his list as one of the coolest days ever!

During their first few weekends in South Carolina, the Brinkleys would climb in the car and explore the neighboring cities. Max liked the hustle and bustle of Columbia. There was so much to do there.

In Columbia, Knox got a chance to go the science museum, and the twins were super excited at the zoo. They giggled as they fed the giraffes. Max's favorite thing? Riding the zoo carousel. Of course, he didn't dare tell anyone he loved carousel rides. After all, he was in middle school. He was almost an adult. Instead, being the most awesome big brother on Earth, Max agreed to ride the carousel with his sisters so his mom could relax on the sidelines.

That same day, quite by accident, and possibly because he was lost, Dad drove past a large mall. Mom almost poked Dad in the eye pointing to it. Needless to say, the family wandered around the mall for at least three hours while Max complained about his feet hurting and Knox begged to find a nice coffee shop where he could do some reading.

On this particular Saturday, though, the

Brinkleys decided a staycation was in order—complete with popcorn, candy, and a movie. Even though it was late afternoon, everyone was already in pajamas. Mom thought it would be nice if everyone would wear the pajamas that Grandma Vera had sent them for Christmas. Max protested because she'd sent him footed pajamas with ponies all over them.

"You realize that this is humiliating, right?" Max questioned his mother. "No self-respecting eleven-year-old dresses in ponies."

"You look quite adorable," she said with a smile.

"Agorrable," the twins said as they attempted to mimic Mom.

"See! Even toddlers know I look silly," Max pouted.

"Nonsense," Mom said. She stretched her arms out. "Come sit next to me. The movie's about to start."

It was Knox's turn to pick the movie. Another musical. Max was less than thrilled.

Halfway through the movie, just as Max began to doze off during another dance number, the doorbell rang.

Dad, who was munching away on popcorn, put down the bowl. "I'll get it," he said. As he opened the door, everyone turned to see the unexpected guest.

No one was there.

Dad stepped outside. Max's ears perked up. He could hear Dad yelling at someone.

"Okay, this isn't funny! Don't ring our doorbell again!" Dad hollered. He slammed the door.

"What happened, Carter?" Mom asked.

"All I could see was someone running away. Whoever it was ran between the houses, toward the wooded area. Looked like a young kid. I'm sure it was just a prank," he said.

"It's called a ding-dong ditch, Dad," Max spoke up.

"Yeah, yeah. No big deal. Let's get back to the movie." He ushered his family back into the living room. Knox and Max sat on the rug.

Knox whispered in Max's ear. "You think it was the same person who rang the doorbell a few weeks ago?"

Max shrugged. "I don't know."

"There is a high probability that it's the same person," Knox said.

Something in his brother's tone got Max's attention. Knox was proposing a challenge. A good, old-fashioned sleuthing challenge, like something straight out of a detective book. Max smirked. If there was a mystery to be solved, he and his super-genius brother were the right men for the job.

"Knox?"

"Yeah, Max?" Knox asked eagerly.

"Pass me the popcorn."

Knox handed the bowl to his brother. Shoving a handful of popcorn into his mouth, Max muttered, "Mysteries are cool."

"Totally," Knox said with a smile.

CHAPTER 6

DON'T MESS WITH
THE NEEDLEMEYER

The Brinkleys weren't the only victims of the recent ding-dong ditches. Neighbors from almost every house in the neighborhood were abuzz about the mysterious shadowy figure that managed to scurry away into the night after ringing the doorbells.

Their heavily wooded neighborhood was the perfect target for a ding-dong ditcher. It was flanked on one side by trees and marshes. Many houses were separated by rows of mature trees. It would be easy for a ding-dong ditcher to escape into the woods without being noticed.

Some neighbors dismissed the ditching as harmless fun, while others said it warranted police action. Mrs. Needlemeyer, a rather cross older woman whose smile Max said was permanently upside down, let everyone know that if she got hold of the "hooligan," she'd teach him a thing or two about respecting others.

Max believed her.

Since the mysterious doorbell ringing was big news for the neighborhood, a special meeting had been called. Dad had to work late, so Mom had taken the kids to the meeting. At least forty neighbors had gathered to discuss their concerns. Some thought it was a group of children ringing the doorbells. Others guessed it was the work of one lone culprit.

"Regardless of who it is, there will be consequences when he's found," Mrs. Needlemeyer said. "This has to be nipped in the bud!"

Mr. Martinez, who lived two houses down from Mrs. Needlemeyer, spoke up. "What kind of consequences? It's probably just a kid playing a harmless prank."

Mrs. Needlemeyer glared at Mr. Martinez.

"There is nothing harmless about making me miss *Lawrence Welk*," she said.

"Huh?" Mr. Martinez asked, with a puzzled look on his face. But Mrs. Needlemeyer was done listening to reason.

"The rest of you can sit here and make excuses if you want. When I get my hands on the person responsible for this, you can believe the first thing I'm going to do is call the police," she said, shaking her fist. "The next time that hooligan rings my doorbell and runs will be his last. I'll teach whoever it is to disturb me and Lawrence Welk."

Max whispered to his mom. "Is Lawrence Welk Mrs. Needlemeyer's boyfriend?"

His mom chuckled. "No, Max. It's an old television show. I wouldn't want to be the person responsible for making her miss it."

"Me either," Max said. "I think messing with Mrs. Needlemeyer is like dangling a cookie in front of a hungry dog."

"I agree with you on this one, Max," Mom said.

A few days later, Knox and Max were discussing Mrs. Needlemeyer.

"I heard that her cat doesn't even meow anymore," Knox said.

"What? Knox, that's so silly," Max laughed.

"My friend Wyatt said a woman who works at the vet's office told his aunt that Mrs. Needlemeyer yelled so much at her cat about meowing that the cat must have decided to just stop doing it."

"She is pretty scary," Max said.

While Mrs. Needlemeyer did not wear a smile, she did wear a different muumuu every day of the week. Max had never seen anyone wear such brightly colored, shapeless dresses. Green muumuus. Polka-dot muumuus. Light-blue-with-white-buttons-down-the-front muumuus. Max wondered if she shopped at an online store with a name like "Muumuus "R" Us." She also wore black horn-rimmed glasses, which were always propped on top of her head. Before she began any conversation, she slid those glasses down to the tip of her nose and glared out of them. Everyone in the neighborhood said she couldn't see a thing without those glasses.

Max and Knox tried their best to stay off of Mrs. Needlemeyer's radar, but Dad insisted they ask her at least a couple of times a week if she needed help around the house. Without fail, she'd find something for the pair to do.

"You two boys respect your elders. You'll grow up and do something with your lives," she said every time they came over. "A little hard work never hurt anybody."

Max couldn't stand going over to Mrs. Needlemeyer's house to do chores. There were a million things he'd rather be doing. But Knox didn't seem to mind it. He confided in Max once that he secretly found Mrs. Needlemeyer very intriguing. To him, she was living history.

"Were you married?" Knox asked her one day while he was dusting the figurines on one of her shelves. Mrs. Needlemeyer paused, put her hands on her hips, and sighed.

"I did have a husband. His name was Joel. He got himself killed in the Vietnam War. But that was a long time ago. No use in dredging up the past," she said with a sigh.

Without saying another word, Knox walked over to her and hugged her. Mrs. Needlemeyer seemed stunned. Max, who was feeding the cat, stood still and watched as Mrs. Needlemeyer hugged his brother with one hand. But as quickly as the embrace began, it ended.

Mrs. Needlemeyer cleared her throat and composed herself.

"Was Vietnam before or after the Civil War?" Max chimed in. Knox laughed out loud at his brother. Mrs. Needlemeyer put her hands on her hips and shook her head. Max felt puzzled. He was sure Mrs. Needlemeyer was old enough to remember the Civil War—even if she may have been a little girl back then.

"That question does not even deserve a response," she said. "Get back to work. Those figurines can't dust themselves." The boys could hear the grumpiness in her voice. "You come over here to work, not to ask a million questions. Be seen, not heard, that's what I always say." Her voice trailed away.

She had been on a rampage since the suspected ding-dong ditcher struck her home. She was especially annoyed because she had been in the middle of watching a rerun of *The Lawrence Welk Show*. She watched it every Saturday evening while she ate a steak dinner.

"Those were the days," Mrs. Needlemeyer would say when talking about her favorite show. "That's before the world went straight to a big old garbage bin."

Max had this much to say about the ding-dong ditcher: whoever it was had a lot of nerve picking a fight with Mrs. Needlemeyer.

CHAPTER 7

KEEP YOUR FOUR EYES ON THE BALL

After a couple of failed tests and a teacher's observation that Max seemed to be straining to see the Smart Board, his mom scheduled an eye exam. Max was mortified when the optometrist confirmed that he needed glasses. Today was the dreaded pickup day. All he could think of was Celia and the other kids calling him "four-eyes." He felt sick.

"Let's not be hasty. There HAS to be another solution. What about an eye transplant?" Max said glumly.

"I think glasses are the better option," Dr. Jenkins said with a laugh as he made the final adjustments to the glasses. "And you only have to wear them when you're reading."

"Thank goodness," Max sighed as he looked at himself in the mirror.

"You look very handsome, Max," said Mom.

"You're my mom. You have to say that."

Dr. Jenkins handed Max a protective pouch containing his new glasses. Max wasted no time hiding them away in his book bag.

He returned to school just in time for history. And it was just his luck that his teacher asked him to read a passage aloud. Max froze. What should he do? Take out his glasses and possibly face ridicule from his classmates? Pretend he had no new glasses and take the chance of messing up while reading out loud? Without giving it much more thought, Max whipped the glasses out of his backpack and began to read. To his relief, the room was silent. He easily read aloud his section about the Great Depression without making one mistake. Mrs. Turner praised his excellent reading.

Max was all smiles. Nothing could ruin his day! In fact, his celebrating continued into PE when he learned that the class would be playing dodgeball—his favorite sport of all time. He had been the dodgeball champ at his old school.

Coach Phillips chose him and Hector to be team captains. Celia shot Max a dirty look when he chose Finn Harper to be on his team. Max didn't care. Finn looked like he could hold his own in dodgeball.

As soon as Coach Phillips blew his whistle, the thunder of running feet began to pound the gym floor. Max grabbed a ball and immediately tagged Malcolm Smith. A second later, a ball whizzed by Max's head. Hector had missed! Another ball sailed right for Max, but he caught it. Tyrell Daniels was out.

When Max finally got a chance to look around, he could see that only three of Hector's teammates were still in the game. He could smell VICTORY!

A loose ball! Max ran for it, but Celia quickly snatched it up. Even though she was wearing a wicked grin, Max couldn't help but think how absolutely adorable she looked with her hair pulled back in a neat ponytail. Celia had only one thing on her mind, though.

"Guess you weren't quick enough, four-eyes," she called with a sneer.

Before she could hit Max, though, Celia was tagged out by a ball that seemed to come out of nowhere. Max looked around and saw Amber giving Finn a high five. Finn had saved him!

Celia stomped over to her team's side of the bleachers. It wasn't long before the rest of her team was sitting beside her. Max was still the reigning dodgeball champion.

The bell rang, and the class scurried to get in line. Max stood next to Finn.

"Good game! That throw was pretty awesome!" Max said.

"It was nothing. I was the dodgeball champ at my old school," Finn replied.

"No way! I was too. It's my favorite thing to do other than play Dungeon Creator."

Finn's eyes lit up at the mention of the video game.

"That's my favorite game of all time! I just discovered a new dungeon on level 19," Finn said excitedly. Max was impressed.

"Will you tell me the coordinates?"

"Sure. I'll add you to my friends list after school."

Finn began to glance around then, scanning the bleachers as if looking for someone or something. "I forgot my hoodie."

Mrs. Rice had entered the gym, and the line began to move. Finn got out of line and began to search the gym.

One of the coaches noticed Finn searching and came over. "Someone's probably taken it to the lost-and-found box in the office," he assured Finn. "Can you describe the hoodie?"

Finn scowled. "It's a dark blue zip-up hoodie with an eagle across the front. My mom sent that hoodie to me. I've got to find it."

The coach suggested he check the lost-and-found after classes let out for the day. Finn sighed, and reluctantly got back into the line, which began to move toward lunch.

Within a few minutes, Finn was smiling again as he and Max resumed their conversation about their favorite games. No matter what the other kids thought, Max was sure he'd just made a new friend.

CHAPTER 8

A SUSPECT
REVEALED

It turned out that Max and his new best friend, Finn, had more than their passion for dodgeball and Dungeon Creator in common. Finn was an Air Force kid who had lived all over the world. His parents were dual military, meaning both of his parents were in the military. Finn's mother was currently deployed to Kuwait. His grandmother had moved in with them to help his dad during the nine-month deployment.

"All of the kids think you're some kind of juvenile delinquent," Max said matter-of-factly.

Finn snorted. "Yeah, I know. I think it's kind of funny. If they won't take the time to get to know me, they can think whatever they want."

"Doesn't it bother you that they say things about you that aren't true?" Max asked.

Finn shook his head.

"No. It doesn't matter to me. This is just like the three other schools I've been to since kindergarten. It's a stop on the map," Finn sighed. "My parents will both get deployed again, and I'll have to go stay with my grandma or my aunt. I'll be alone again with no friends."

Max punched Finn lightly on the arm.

"I'm your friend," Max said with a smile. "And we should make a pact to stay in touch. When we're thirty-five, we should meet at Disney World with our wives and kids. That would be so cool."

Finn laughed.

"That would be pretty cool. You promise?"

Max extended his hand. "I promise."

Even though most of the kids at school thought Max had lost it because he liked hanging out with Finn, Max didn't care. Max thought of Finn as his "battle buddy": someone who understood how rough military life could be for kids and who would stick up for him no matter what. Finn was Shaggy to Max's Scooby Doo. Totally.

But a chilly evening in April almost changed

all of that.

Off-and-on spring showers had made it a very lazy Sunday, and the Brinkleys were enjoying a board game marathon. As usual, Mom was emerging as the big winner. Max was beginning to feel like a sore loser. Just as he was about to redeem himself in a matching game, a loud commotion outside grabbed everyone's attention. Dad went running for the door.

The sun was setting, and the streetlights had begun to flicker on. From the doorway, Max could see Mrs. Needlemeyer, gesturing excitedly as she talked to a police officer on her front porch. Neighbors had begun to gather in front of her house. The Brinkleys hurried to join them.

"What happened?" Dad asked as they crossed into her yard. There was a broken flowerpot on the front porch, and her prized picture window was shattered.

"I'll tell you what happened! I had my hands on that little troublemaker," Mrs. Needlemeyer said angrily as she waved what looked like a piece of clothing in the air. "He managed to wiggle out of his jacket, and he ran away from me."

The police officer attempted to calm her down. "I know you're upset, Mrs. Needlemeyer, but I need you to tell me exactly what happened."

Mrs. Needlemeyer cleared her throat.

"Well, I was just about to make my famous prune cobbler when I heard a tiny tapping sound out front. I looked out and saw that juvenile delinquent throwing rocks at the flowerpot I had sitting on my railing. His aim must have been bad, or else I scared him when I came running out, because he hit my window and broke it," she said. "I ran down in enough time to grab him and pull him onto the porch so I could call the police. He started trying to get away from me and bumped into my beautiful flowerpot. That's when I lost my grip and the scoundrel ran away!"

"Did you a good look at the suspect?" the police officer asked.

"Of course I did. It was a boy. He couldn't have been any more than thirteen years old," Mrs. Needlemeyer said. "And I still have his jacket!"

As she passed the garment she'd been holding to the police officer, it unfurled to reveal an eagle, silvery in the lamplight. Max gasped. It was Finn's hoodie!

CHAPTER 9

SHERLOCK KNOX

Finn was in trouble. All of the evidence seemed to point to him as the notorious, brazen ding-dong ditcher. The next morning in homeroom, Max waited eagerly for Finn to arrive so they could talk about the incident at Mrs. Needlemeyer's house. He was still waiting when the bell rang and class started. Finn wasn't coming.

"We tried to tell you that kid was bad news," Hector said to Max during PE. "You didn't want to listen. I guess you'll be visiting him in prison this summer."

"He's not going to prison," Max shot back indignantly. "He didn't do it."

"Sure he didn't," Hector laughed. "Grow up, Max. That kid is trouble with a capital T."

Max was getting tired of hearing people talk about Finn. There had to be an explanation for all of this. Max was glad his parents hadn't told him to give up on his friendship with Finn. He hoped they could help him figure out what was going on.

"It's best we stay out of it and let his family sort this one out," Dad said at the dinner table that night. "Finn seems like a pretty good kid. If he did this, though, he has to be held responsible for his actions."

"But Dad," Max protested, "Finn couldn't have done it. He didn't even have his hoodie anymore! He lost it in gym class last week."

Max described the whole scenario: how Finn had looked everywhere in the gym, how upset he'd been, and how the teacher had told him to check the lost-and-found.

"Did he?" Dad asked.

"Did he what?"

"Did he check lost-and-found and get it back?"

Max frowned. He'd never asked Finn if he'd

gotten his prized hoodie back. In fact, until last night, he'd forgotten all about it. Some friend he was!

Max sighed. "I don't know. But I don't think so. I hadn't seen him wear it since. Plus, Dad, I just *can't* believe Finn would do it. He's a really good guy. He's my battle buddy!"

Dad put his hand on Max's shoulder. "If you believe in him, Max, I do too."

"Me too!" Knox chimed in.

Max jumped from his chair. "We've got to prove he didn't do this! His punishment is going to include doing community service work at Mrs. Needlemeyer's house for the entire summer. That's worse than going to juvenile detention!"

"I don't know if there's much we can do, big guy," Dad said. "They have his jacket as evidence, and Mrs. Needlemeyer pointed him out."

Knox shook his head. "Dad, Finn is innocent until proven guilty. Mrs. Needlemeyer may seem to be a credible eyewitness, but there may be more going on here than meets the eye."

Max had no idea what his little brother was talking about, but he liked it.

"I take it you have a plan?"

"I do," said Knox. "And we need to get started

right now before any clues disappear."

"This is all very intriguing," Mom said.

"Mom, can we go outside for a little while?" Knox asked.

"It's okay with me. Sounds like you two have some work to do," she said with a smile.

"Let's go!" Max exclaimed.

"Are you skipping dessert tonight, Max? That's not like you," Dad said.

"Well, I guess it can wait a *few* minutes," Max laughed as he settled back into his chair.

After eating a big piece of Mom's homemade pecan pie each, Max and Knox put on their rain boots. It was still muddy from all the recent rain. Knox carried a small backpack with him.

"What's in there?" Max asked.

"The essentials for any investigation— flashlights and a digital camera," Knox answered.

Max loved having such a smart brother.

"Lead the way," Max said as they headed out of the door.

"Don't stay out too late. You've got school tomorrow," Mom said.

When Knox began to cross the street in the direction of Mrs. Needlemeyer's house, Max stopped in his tracks. He remembered how furious she had been the night before. A furious Mrs. Needlemeyer was even worse than a grumpy Mrs. Needlemeyer.

"There is no way I am going over there of my own free will. No way," Max said.

Knox stared at his brother.

"Do you want to help your friend or not? If there are clues, they're in Mrs. Needlemeyer's yard. That's the last place the ditcher's been," Knox said. "Plus, Mrs. Needlemeyer isn't even home. I heard Mom on the phone with her this afternoon, saying we'd keep an eye on her place while she stays overnight at her sister's in Florence."

"Okay, okay," Max said hesitantly.

Knox handed Max a flashlight. As they approached the house, Max saw that the broken flowerpot had been cleared away, and where the picture window had been, there was now a big piece of plywood nailed in place.

"I'll search one side of her yard, and you look on the other. Look for any clues that may tell us who was here the other night," Knox said.

The yard was huge. Max really had no idea what they were looking for, but he wasn't going to tell Knox that. He walked slowly, shoving the flashlight into random bushes that lined Mrs. Needlemeyer's house. He hoped his dad hadn't gotten a good look at those bushes, because Max was sure he would be the one to have to come over and trim them. Ugh. Nothing there. He shined a light into the grass. Nothing there either.

He was relieved when his brother called out to him.

"Hey, Max! I think I've found something!"

Max ran over to Knox, who was kneeling down at the edge of a flowerbed, shining a light onto a patch of mud.

"There's an impression here in the mud—a footprint," Knox said with grin.

"It's probably Mrs. Needlemeyers footprint," Max said. "She stomps around out here all the time."

"Nope, the probability of that is very slim. Mrs. Needlemeyer wears slippers most of the day. Those slippers would hardly make an imprint with ridges in it like this. And besides, her foot would be bigger," Knox said.

The kid probably has something there, Max thought.

"By shining this light source diagonally on the ground, I can see the ridges of an impression,"

Knox said as he snapped a photo of it. "I think we should make a mold of this print."

Max peered at the print. "Wow, that's pretty cool! Do you think this could be the footprint of the ding-dong ditcher?"

"I don't know yet, but I hope so!" Knox said. "Stay here. I'm going home to get some plaster of Paris and water so we can make a mold."

Max didn't even bother asking why his brother had plaster lying around. It was just the sort of weird thing he would expect of Knox. "Okay. I'll stay here, but hurry back. It's super creepy over here," Max said.

Five minutes later, Knox returned with the plaster and other supplies. He measured the print, made a mold of it, and then sat patiently waiting for it to dry. He then put the casting in a shoebox he'd brought from the house.

"Looks like a tennis shoe print to me. What size shoe does Finn wear?" Knox asked.

Max thought for a moment. "I'm not sure, but his feet are definitely bigger than mine. That kid is *tall*."

Without speaking, Knox lifted the new casting and laid it on the ground beside his brother's foot. It was about half an inch shorter than the length of Max's sneaker.

"Max, this footprint is too small to have been made by a man's shoe." Knox looked around. "There has got to be something else here," he said.

Just then, the boys heard their mom calling for them from across the street.

"We've got to go, Knox. Let's come back tomorrow," Max said.

"No! Five more minutes, Max! There's something here. I know it."

The boys grabbed their flashlights and again began to look around the yard. Max ran to the back gate and scanned the perimeter with his light. He was about to give up when a tiny speck of white in the grass caught his eye. He hurried toward it. Could the ditcher have lost a tooth in his struggle with Mrs. Needlemeyer?

Max reached down and picked up something small and round and smooth. He had to catch his breath. He couldn't believe it.

"Knox!" Max screamed. "I think I know who did it!"

CHAPTER 10

HOW TO CATCH A DING-DONG DITCHER

Besides the last day of school, middle school field day was the second-most eagerly anticipated day of the year. What could be better than spending all day long outside playing games? Competing was definitely Max's thing. He was in sixth-grade-boy heaven.

Today, though, Max had more on his mind than winning at tug-of-war or knocking over bowling pins. He knew the identity of the ding-dong ditcher, and it was time to reel the culprit in.

At lunchtime, all the middle school classes headed into the gym. Max grabbed a sandwich, chips, and a soda. He looked into the bleachers. Finn was sitting alone at the top. Max didn't like seeing his friend so lonely, but instead of joining him, he began scanning the bleachers for other familiar faces.

Hector and Jonathan were chatting in the middle of a sea of kids. Celia and her friends sat one row above them. Max waved at Hector, and Hector moved over to make room for him.

Celia glared at Max as he took a seat.

"There's more room up there where your loser friend is sitting," she sneered. Max grimaced.

"Leave me alone, okay? He's not my friend anymore."

Celia raised her eyebrows.

"Really? Well, I can't say I blame you. After all, he is a criminal, for goodness' sake. I hope your parents would teach you better than to hang around common criminals."

Max turned to her.

"Can you keep a secret?" he asked.

She smiled and moved closer. "Of course!"

Max's heart was racing. Even though she was SUPER mean, he still thought she was the prettiest girl he'd ever seen.

"Well, Finn is in big trouble for all of that ding-dong ditching he was doing in our neighborhood. His parents are so mad they're thinking of sending him to military school."

Celia gasped.

"Mrs. Needlemeyer doesn't think that's enough punishment, though. She's got it in for him. She's not going to stop until she ruins his life," Max said glumly.

Celia laughed.

"Oh, please. No one is afraid of Mrs. Needlemeyer. She is so full of hot air!"

Max shook his head.

"I used to think the same thing, but this time is different. She's really upset. In fact, she told my mom that if anyone ever tried to ding-dong ditch her again, she would make sure people would be SORRY," Max said.

Celia sat straight up.

"Oh, really? Just what is she going to do?"

Max shrugged his shoulders.

"I don't know. She knows that Finn is the one responsible for all of this trouble. It's almost like she's daring him to come back and try it again. If I were him, I wouldn't chance it. No one can go up against Mrs. Needlemeyer," Max said.

Celia stood up.

"A dare? I don't think she should dare him. I mean, after all, he is a common criminal." Max could see that Celia was deep in thought.

"I think you're right, Celia. Mrs. Needlemeyer is full of hot air. She just thinks she can scare us kids," he said.

"That old lady doesn't scare me at all!" Celia stomped her foot and stepped down from the bleachers. She looked back at Max.

"If I were Finn, I'd teach her a lesson." And with that, she walked out of the gym.

Hector elbowed Max. "What was that all about?" he asked. Max smiled at him.

"Oh, nothing. Celia was just telling me about her plans for the weekend," he said.

Without really meaning to, Hector changed the subject.

"Where did my hat go? It was sitting right here."

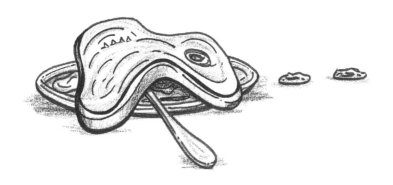

CHAPTER 11

THE "STEAK" OUT

On the way home from school, Max told Knox he thought it was a good time to pay Mrs. Needlemeyer a visit. Knox agreed.

But Mrs. Needlemeyer seemed surprised to see them.

"I don't need help with anything today, boys. Go home," she said, starting to close the door.

Max spoke up.

"Wait! Mrs. Needlemeyer, we have something we'd like to talk to you about."

Mrs. Needlemeyer took her glasses from atop her head and peered at the boys.

"Make it quick. My court shows are coming on

in half an hour," she grumbled. She led them into her living room.

"Mrs. Needlemeyer, we think we know who caused the damage on your front porch," Max said.

Mrs. Needlemeyer stared at Max. "I know, too. It was that punk kid with the blue hoodie. Listen, boys, did you come over here to waste my time? This ship has sailed," she said.

"We have evidence that indicates someone else did it, Mrs. Needlemeyer," Knox said. "We want your help to catch the real person responsible." He walked over to her. "Mrs. Needlemeyer, were you wearing your glasses that evening?"

"Of course. I always have my glasses on," she answered.

"Were your glasses on top of your head, or on your face?" Knox continued.

Mrs. Needlemeyer paused to think.

"They were on top of my head," she said.

"Mrs. Needlemeyer, you've said yourself that you can't see a thing without your glasses," Knox said. "So it's possible that you really didn't see what you thought you saw."

Mrs. Needlemeyer huffed.

"How do you explain the hoodie, Kojak?"

"Who's Kojak?" Max asked.

Mrs. Needlemeyer let out a hearty laugh. Max was shocked. He'd never heard her laugh before.

"Kojak was the name of the title character in a 1970s detective TV show. Kojak was smooth and could solve any crime," she said.

She patted Knox on the top of his head.

"Okay, okay. You've got my attention, and I'm listening. It sounds like you two having been giving all of this a lot of thought," she said.

"We found some clues in your yard, Mrs. Needlemeyer. Max and I are sure that Finn didn't ding-dong ditch anyone," Knox said.

Max spoke up. "Yeah, but we think we know who did. We need your help, though."

Mrs. Needlemeyer put a finger to her lip.

"This could be interesting," she said, rubbing her chin. "I assume you have a plan?"

"We want to have a stakeout!" Max blurted in excitement.

Knox stepped in to explain: "We have reason to believe the hooligan will return to the scene of the crime this weekend."

"This weekend? Oh, no, that's not a good time for me. Saturday is my day for steak and *Lawrence Welk*."

"You could always eat your steak during our

stakeout," Knox giggled. "It's highly probable that we may need to sleep over. There's no telling how long the stakeout will last."

Mrs. Needlemeyer scowled, and Max shot a worried look in his brother's direction. "There is nothing funny about the possibility of me missing *Lawrence Welk*," she said.

"If we make you miss it, I promise to come watch it with you next weekend," Knox begged.

And like that, Mrs. Needlemeyer's heart seemed to soften.

"I'm going to hold you to that, young man," she said. She began to walk them to the door. "So, get me the details of this so-called stakeout, and we'll go from there. But for now—get out."

And she closed the door.

Max gave his brother a high five.

"We've got this, little bro," Max said. "Bring it on, ding-dong ditcher!"

CHAPTER 12

DING-DONG!
WE KNOW WHO'S THERE!

"You want to spend the night at Mrs. Needlemeyer's this weekend?" Max's mom didn't know what to make of her boys' strange request.

"She said we could if it was okay with you and Dad," Max pleaded.

"There has to be something more to all of this that I'm not getting," Mom said.

Max touched his mom's shoulder.

"Mrs. Needlemeyer is helping us with something important," he said. "We might be really close to solving our very first mystery!"

"This is so cool," Knox said.

Mom glanced at both of them. "Well, if she

said it's okay..."

Sensing that she was giving in, Max poked his bottom lip out and began to beg. "She's just across the street. We'll have adult supervision, mind our manners, and try not to make her miss *Lawrence Welk*. Mom, PLEASE!"

Just as she was about to answer, sounds from the nanny cam grabbed her attention. Heidi and Harley were waking from their naps.

Mom turned to Max. "If you boys promise not to bother Mrs. Needlemeyer too much..."

"We promise!" Max and Knox said in unison.

"It's okay with me," Mom said as she headed for the stairs to the twins' room. "I think it will be a good thing for Mrs. Needlemeyer to have some company. She has to get lonely living all by herself."

Max shivered.

"That is so gross," he said, closing his eyes tight and sticking out his tongue. "Who would want to live with her? She gives me the creeps! I hope I survive this weekend."

Knox gave his brother a stern look.

"She's really not that bad. Like Mom said, she's lonely. And I think she's just misunderstood—sort of like Finn. People haven't taken the time to get to know Finn or Mrs. Needlemeyer; that's why no one understands them."

As usual, Max knew his little brother was right. He felt bad for what he'd said about Mrs. Needlemeyer.

"Hey, Knox?"

"Yes?"

"I'm glad you're my brother."

"Ditto."

"Let's start packing the things we'll need this weekend. Don't want to forget anything," Max said.

"Sounds good," Knox said. "Also, Mom just gave me a great idea. We're going to need the nanny cam."

When Mrs. Needlemeyer opened the door, Max hoped she couldn't see the surprised looks on their faces.

Mrs. Needlemeyer was wearing a pair of blue jeans and a University of Alabama T-shirt. *She actually looks NORMAL,* Max thought.

"Well, don't stand there staring. Come on in," she said. She pointed them in the direction of the living room.

"I couldn't very well go on a stakeout in my

housedress. I thought this outfit was more appropriate," she said.

"We think you look very nice," Knox said politely.

The smell of steak sizzling on a griddle permeated the house. "You boys go take a seat while I finish up dinner. I told your mother I'd like to treat you to a steak dinner tonight."

It was only a few minutes before Mrs. Needlemeyer served them a dinner of steak, loaded baked potatoes, and squash.

"This all looks delicious, Mrs. Needlemeyer. Thank you so much," Max said.

Mrs. Needlemeyer nodded, her mouth full of food. Then she swallowed.

"I don't get too many guests around here, so I figured it would be a great time to cook for someone else. *Lawrence Welk* comes on in half an hour and it's getting dark outside, so I'll need to know your plan."

"Well, we'll need to set up the nanny cam so we can easily view your front door. That way, we'll be able to see the ding-dong ditcher when he makes his move," Knox said. "We'll also have to keep very quiet, so it looks like you're the only one home. I suggest we watch *Lawrence Welk* in one of the back rooms, so we can talk without the ditcher hearing us."

Mrs. Needlemeyer managed a smile.

"Sounds good to me," she said. "Finish your dinner, and we'll get to work!"

The threesome laughed and shared stories during dinner. Knox recounted the time when he was two years old and accidentally locked his family outside during a downpour. Max laughed about the time he shaved his eyebrows off while his mother was sleeping. Mrs. Needlemeyer told them about the time she convinced all of her eighth-grade classmates to take the desks out of the classroom while their teacher was out of the room. She warned them against such behavior, though.

"Wow, that's pretty cool," Max said. "It's hard to think of you as a kid."

Mrs. Needlemeyer rested her arms on the table.

"Well, it definitely didn't happen yesterday. So many things happened a long time ago," she said. She got up to clear the table and glanced at the clock on the wall.

"*Lawrence Welk* time!"

The boys grabbed their bags. "I'll go set up the nanny cam," Knox said.

Max helped Mrs. Needlemeyer take the dishes to the sink. She then turned on a single lamp in the front room to show the ditcher she was home.

"I feel like a secret agent," Mrs. Needlemeyer giggled.

As the show began, the boys plopped onto a light blue love seat, and Mrs. Needlemeyer took a seat on her bed.

"What's with all the bubbles?" Max asked.

"There's a bubble machine that blows toward the orchestra at the beginning of the show," Mrs. Needlemeyer said.

"Did you and your husband use to watch this show?"

Mrs. Needlemeyer was quiet for a moment. She sighed.

"We did like to watch this show together. Sometimes we'd dance. Joel was a good dancer. I can't say the same for myself. I was cursed with two left feet," she laughed.

"Is that why you're so mad all the time—because you have two left feet? I bet that hurts," Max said with concern. Knox elbowed him.

"What? Did I miss something?"

"That's a saying, Max. There is no way Mrs. Needlemeyer could really have two left feet," Knox said.

"Oh, I get it. That's funny, Mrs. Needlemeyer," Max laughed. "Knox is a pretty good dancer too. I don't think anyone on this show is a breakdancer, though."

"I'll have to teach Knox how to polka one of these days," Mrs. Needlemeyer said. "Now, that's dancing! Stand up; let me show you a few moves!"

She grabbed Knox's arms and whirled him around the room. Max clapped, and the dancing couple bowed.

"Did your husband polka?" Knox asked.

"He could polka. I think he even taught me. But that was so long ago. Things were different back then."

"Your husband was in the military like our dad," Knox said. Mrs. Needlemeyer nodded.

"He was in the Army—just like your dad."

Max looked at Mrs. Needlemeyer.

"You told us that your husband was killed in the Vietnam War. Our dad has been deployed to Iraq and Afghanistan, and I was scared he wouldn't come back either," Max said. He could feel tears pricking his eyes. That always happened when he thought about his dad not coming home from deployment.

Mrs. Needlemeyer came to sit next to the boys.

"It's okay to be scared. You wouldn't be human if you weren't scared of some things. But don't you worry, your dad will always come back."

"How do you know that? How does anyone know that?" Max asked.

"I'm an old lady. I know things," Mrs. Needlemeyer said.

She pointed to a picture on the nightstand next to her bed. "That's my Joel, and he has always been here with me, even after all these years. He was killed July 1, 1967. He crawled out of a foxhole during a mortar attack to save his best friend. I found out he died on my twenty-fourth birthday. That was more than forty-five years ago."

"Wow... You've been alive for a really long time," Max said.

Mrs. Needlemeyer couldn't help but laugh.

"Max, you really know how to lighten the mood," she said. "I'm really not that old. I'll probably be around to be at your college graduation."

"If you say so!" Max laughed. "That would be a miracle–"

Knox put his hand over his brother's mouth.

"Shh… You guys, I think I heard something," Knox whispered. "Let's check the nanny cam!"

Knox held up the device. They could see the fuzzy image of a person standing on the front porch.

"The ding-dong ditcher is out there!"

Mrs. Needlemeyer's stern face returned.

"He is *not* going to get away with it this time," she said as she stormed out of the room, with Max and Knox following.

"We've got to remain calm, Mrs. Needlemeyer, or the ditcher *will* get away. You head out the side door; Max and I will head out the back," Knox said.

The threesome crept slowly through the house, avoiding any windows. By the time they opened the side and back doors, they could hear that someone was outside.

"Stay as close as you can to the bushes," Knox advised.

The doorbell rang. A second later, Mrs. Needlemeyer pounced.

"You won't get away this time, you little punk!" she said as sprung from the bushes.

A shadowy figure in a sweatshirt and hat started, stumbling a little before regaining its balance. Then the ditcher jumped from the porch and began to run.

"They're headed for the trees!" Knox shouted.

Mrs. Needlemeyer was fast for an older woman, but Max was faster. He trailed right behind the dark figure around the corner of the house, several paces ahead of Mrs. Needlemeyer and his little brother.

By the time they'd reached the edge of the backyard, Max had just managed to grab ahold of his target's sweatshirt when the ditcher jerked left, yanking free and sending Max flying onto his chest in the wet grass. He leapt up just as the others reached him, and the chase continued into the neighboring yard.

"Get back here!" Mrs. Needlemeyer screamed. "That slippery scoundrel will disappear into the woods!"

Through three patchy hedges and two backyards, the four ran. But now the ditcher had a solid lead. When they crossed into Mr. Martinez's yard, Max saw the shadowy form of a football lying in the grass directly in his path. He barely had to think. He knew just what to do.

The football made a clean arc in the air, the wet hide gleaming in the light of Mr. Martinez's porch lamp. It struck the ditcher in the back of the head with enough force to knock the kid to the ground, and in an instant, Max, Knox, and Mrs. Needlemeyer were standing over a sprawling, dazed ding-dong ditcher.

All the commotion had begun to rouse the neighbors. Back doors began to open. Mr. Martinez ran outside.

"What's going on?" he yelled.

"Anyone got a flashlight?" Max asked. Knox pulled one from the bag he was carrying.

"Well, let's see who this little hooligan is. I've been waiting to see this face for a while now!" Mrs. Needlemeyer announced. With Knox shining the flashlight, Mrs. Needlemeyer pulled the ditcher up by the arm. The mud-streaked face that turned toward them was very pretty, and very, very angry.

"Well, well, well," Mrs. Needlemeyer said. "I guess I was wrong. It's a little girl!"

Max stared at Celia Honeywell. She glared back. Her dark hair was tucked up under a baseball cap—Hector's baseball cap. And her pearl earrings were missing. But her usual sneer was in place.

"What are you looking at?" Celia snarled, trying to shield her eyes from the light.

"I'm looking at a ding-dong ditcher. I knew you couldn't stay away from a dare," Max said. He dug into his jeans pocket and held out his hand. "And here's your earring back. You left it the last time you were here," he said with a smirk.

Celia snatched the earring from his palm. "Whatever. You're still a loser, and so is your friend."

Instead of feeling triumphant, Max was angry. He was angry that even though Celia had finally been caught, she could not admit she was wrong.

"Why do you have to be so mean? All of this—all the things you do and say at school. Why is it worth it? Why even bother?"

"Because I can, that's why," Celia spat.

Mrs. Needlemeyer was towering over Celia, all the while grimacing with her hands on her hips.

"We'll see if your attitude is so nasty once I'm finished with you. Mr. Martinez? Please call the Honeywells. We have something of theirs." With that, Mrs. Needlemeyer escorted Celia up the steps to Mr. Martinez's house.

Max put his arm around his brother's shoulder. "This case is a wrap, little bro," he said.

"And the wicked princess Celia has been tossed out of the kingdom!" Knox laughed. Max shook his head.

"Nope, she'll be back," Max said. "This one will always come back."

CHAPTER 13

TALE OF A SIXTH-GRADE EVERYTHING

It didn't take long for word to spread of Max's takedown of Celia, the ding-dong ditcher. And it was good to be Max Brinkley!

The first few days, Max got so many slaps on the back that he started dodging them because his back hurt. Celia, who had been sentenced to pulling weeds in Mrs. Needlemeyer's garden for six months, and had to apologize to every neighbor whose house she'd visited, rolled her eyes at Max every chance she got.

Max didn't care, though. He was happy Finn's name was finally cleared. The other sixth-grade boys had even started hanging out with Finn, especially since he was Max's best friend. Finn cleared up all of the rumors: He'd never stolen a car or run away. He traveled all the time because his parents were both in the military. Sometimes that meant he had to go live with his grandmother or aunt in other parts of the country.

"Man, that must be hard. I've heard of kids having one parent in the military, but not both parents," Hector said to Finn one day during P.E.

"It can be tough, especially when they're both gone. But I know they would be with me if they could. I'm pretty proud of them," Finn said.

Max joined them. "Being a military brat can be downright rotten, but the cool thing is that there are so many of us around the country and world. It's like a huge club!"

Finn pulled Max to the side.

"I really appreciate everything you did for me. It's nice to have someone stand up for me for once," Finn said. "I'm glad you're my best friend."

"We're not just friends. We're battle buddies. If we can get through sixth grade, we can get through anything," Max said.

There were only three weeks left in the school year. Seventh grade was on the horizon. Feelings of uncertainty were high, because no one really knew what to expect. The coolest thing about seventh grade had to be not being the youngest kids in middle school anymore.

But Max still wasn't thrilled about moving on. He guessed it was the fear of the unknown. His parents always told him that the best way to handle a tough situation was to face it head-on, so that's what he planned to do. As if he had a choice!

But starting the seventh grade was only one source of anxiety for Max. The other? The sixth-grade end-of-the-year dance.

The thought of dancing in front of other people, or dancing with girls, was too much for him. What if he burped or smelled bad? Oh, good grief. He couldn't think about that right now. He decided to handle his issues one at a time. And the first thing on his plate was the school-wide spelling bee.

With Celia getting caught red-handed, the principal had decided an appropriate punishment would be stripping her of her homeroom spelling bee win. She'd no longer be allowed to participate in the school spelling bee. As runner-up, Max would be going in her place to compete with the rest of the sixth-grade class winners for the championship prize of a $25 gift certificate to next year's school book fair. He could hardly have planned a sweeter justice.

The spelling bee was scheduled for the

Wednesday before the end-of-the-year dance, and the whole sixth grade had third period off to attend the sixth-grade competition. After everyone had filed into the gym bleachers and taken their seats, Max and the other contestants lined up on the floor. The vice principal tapped his microphone to call the room to order.

As the vice principal made his opening remarks, Max looked out across the bleachers. He spotted Finn sitting with Hector and the gang, and Finn gave him a thumbs-up. Max smiled back. Then his eyes landed on Celia, sitting a few rows back. She met his gaze with a glare and looked quickly away.

"Maxwell Brinkley."

The vice principal's voice drew Max's attention back.

"You have the first word." Max stepped forward.

"Mr. Brinkley, your word is 'mystery.'"

Max grinned. This was shaping up to be his lucky day.

THE CRUSH MELTS

"So, what does a spelling-bee champion wear to an end-of-the-year dance?" Mom gushed as she looked through Max's closet.

It was Saturday night—the night of the big dance. The twins were sitting nearby in an empty clothes hamper, playing with blocks. Knox was across the street at Mrs. Needlemeyer's house watching *Lawrence Welk*.

Max blushed. "Mom, this is *not* a big deal. It's not the prom or something. I don't have to wear anything too fancy. It's an '80s theme. Mrs. Rice said people used to put together weird patterns and tease their hair. Sounds crazy. I've done some research, though. Mrs. Needlemeyer let me borrow her copy of the movie *Footloose*, so I think I've got some dance moves ready," he said.

"Thank goodness I'm too young to remember much of the '80s," Mom teased. "I bet I can still help you put a totally tubular outfit together, though." Her clothes search continued until she reached the back of the closet.

"Score! I've found just the outfit," she said. "This pink collared shirt Aunt Mindy sent you for Easter is perfect. We can pair it with some worn-out jeans, tease your hair, and you'll be totally '80s." She smiled at her son.

"We'll have to FaceTime with Dad once you get all dressed. We don't want him to miss this," she said. Max's dad was TDY (on Temporary Duty) for a couple of weeks overseas.

Max tried to look serious.

"Okay, Mom, let's talk about how this dance thing is going to work. You are going to drop me and Finn off in front of the school. No taking pictures and no kissy faces. Please, Mom. Promise me."

"Fine," Mom said. "I'll take pics at the front of the school and then I'll be out of there. I still don't know why you wouldn't let me be a chaperone..."

Max's eyes got big. "You will never know how grateful I am that you are not a helicopter mom. Appropriate space and boundaries are appreciated."

Mom smiled. "You've been spending too much time with Knox. You're starting to sound like him."

When she'd taken the twins and gone downstairs, Max put on the pink shirt and jeans and stared in his dresser mirror. Three months had come and gone since his family had left Washington. So much had changed. Heidi and Harley weren't babies anymore. They could play follow-the-leader now. They also knew how to scribble on the walls. Mom wasn't a fan of that milestone.

Knox was teaching Mrs. Needlemeyer to breakdance, and she was teaching him to polka. Neither was any good at their new dance moves, but Max loved to see them try. And even though Max had always loved his little brother, they had become closer since the move. He could tell Knox anything, and Knox was always there to listen.

As for Max, he'd learned that it's okay not to be comfortable in your own skin sometimes. As Dad always said, that skin has got to stretch anyway as you grow up. He'd especially learned that doing the right thing and standing up for others was more important than being comfortable.

Being in this new place had also taught him that he didn't have to lose old friends, but he could always make new ones. He made sure to call his friend Matt in Washington State at least a couple of times a month. Mom encouraged him to also write letters. Max wasn't too fond of the whole writing thing, but he would make an exception for Matt.

His thoughts were interrupted by his mom's voice.

"T-minus fifteen minutes until we need to leave!" she hollered up the stairs. "Come let me do your hair!"

"Okay, Mom!" he answered.

I've got this, Max thought to himself.

Max's mom kept her promise to take only a few pictures in the front of the school. She let Max and Finn know she would be waiting in the pickup line as soon as the dance ended. Max was relieved to see her pull out of the parking lot.

"What do we do now?" Finn asked.

Max flashed a sly grin and busted a move from

Footloose right there on the pavement. "We party."

Finn looked at his friend. "You can be so weird sometimes."

The pair followed their classmates into the gym, which was decorated in tiny white lights and colorful balloons. To the boys' delight, there were classic video game machines lining the wall, and a candy bar filled with all kinds of sweets. They waved to friends who were dancing. Some other kids were participating in a Rubik's cube contest. Finn headed to the candy bar. Max headed to one of the video game machines.

Pac-Man. Sweet! Max loved Pac-Man. He knew where he would be planted for the evening. He could chase ghosts all night.

"Is that a two-player game?" a familiar voice said from behind him. He froze.

"I don't think so," he replied.

"Oh. I was hoping I could play, too. I mean, unless there are hard feelings."

Max turned to face Celia Honeywell. She was dressed in colorful high-top tennis shoes and ripped jeans. Her hair was in pigtails.

"Who are you supposed to be?" Max asked.

"Punky Brewster," Celia said sweetly.

"Oh, never heard of her," Max said as he turned

back to his game.

To Max's disbelief, Celia continued to talk to him.

"Listen, I think we got off on the wrong foot. It was a misunderstanding, that's all."

Max kept playing the game.

"You've been mean to me since day one, Celia. What was there to misunderstand? That you hate me, or REALLY hate me?"

Celia laughed. "I never hated you. I guess I didn't give you a chance. I was wrong about you."

Max hoped that Celia couldn't see how red his ears were getting. Why couldn't she have said this when they first met? Why did she have to try to set Finn up for something he didn't do? Why did she have to be so down-and outright MEAN?

"You were wrong about me, but I think I was wrong about you too," Max said.

"Really? That's so sweet of you to say," she said.

Max faced her.

"I was wrong to think you were a good person," he said flatly.

Celia's smile disappeared. She dropped her head.

"I moved here when I was four years old. My father was in the Air Force. My parents got a divorce when I was seven, and he left us here," she said. "I begged him to take me with him, but he said it would be best if I stayed with my mom."

"I'm sorry, Celia . . ."

Her smile returned.

" . . . but that doesn't give you a right to treat everyone else like dirt," Max said.

Celia's smile turned to a flat line.

"This is what I get for thinking you would understand," she huffed. "You know what? You're just as dumb as I thought you were! I don't know why I'm wasting my time talking to you."

"You know, Celia, I really liked you when I first moved here. I thought you were the most beautiful girl I had ever seen. But the more I got to know you, the more I figured out you weren't as pretty on the inside as you were on the outside. On the inside, I am quite positive you must be filled with slime and hot lava."

Celia stomped her foot.

"How dare you say that to me?" she yelled.

"Because I can." Max smirked.

Celia glowered at him, looking just like a volcano ready to erupt. "You'll be sorry you said that, Max Brinkley."

And with that, Celia Honeywell walked away.

Max felt sorry for her, but something inside him said it was best to let her go.

Finn came running over as the first notes of Michael Jackson's song "Beat It" came on over the speakers.

"What in the heck was that about?" Finn asked.

"Oh, nothing. I finally got something out of my system, and it feels GOOD. I think I'm ready to dance. They're playing my jam!"

Max scanned the room. He walked over to Charlotte Rochester.

"Wanna dance?" he asked.

"Sure," Charlotte answered shyly.

Max danced for the rest of the night. He didn't care that he didn't have rhythm or know many of the '80s songs. He was having fun just being Max Brinkley.

CHAPTER 15

SUMMER VACAY ON THE WAY

It was the first day of summer vacation. Max and Knox were already bored. They were sitting on the porch watching their mom plant flowers around the huge oak tree in the front yard.

"It is so hot out here," Max whined.

"Maxwell, it's only eighty-five degrees. If you think this is hot, wait until August," Mom said.

Knox sighed.

"I miss school already. Maybe I'll go inside and do some practice algebra problems."

Max frowned.

"It's summer. I refuse to think about math or

any other school subject. I also refuse to let you think about schoolwork. Knox, it's just not normal. Stop it, please," Max begged.

"Okay, you two," Mom said. "I promise that you'll have plenty to do this summer." I've already registered you for sports camps and swimming lessons. Don't forget that we're close to the beaches, so I'm sure we'll be spending lots of time by the water. You guys have never been to an ocean warm enough to swim in. It should be a real treat!"

"The beach? Oh no," Max objected. "You know who also likes the beach? SHARKS. No way!"

Knox laughed.

"I read that the probability that a person will get attacked by a shark is like one in 11.5 million. I'm sure you're pretty safe," Knox said.

"Better safe than sorry," Max said.

Mom interrupted.

"You guys, have you seen the lawn gnomes I bought yesterday morning at the gardening store? They were just here a minute ago," she said.

The boys looked around. Potting soil. Plants. No lawn gnomes.

"Mom, I think it would be okay if you don't find them. They're creepy-looking anyways. If you find them, give them to Mrs. Needlemeyer. She likes creepy stuff," Max said.

"Very funny. I wonder where those gnomes are?" Knox leapt to his feet.

"Another mystery! Are you up for it, Max?" Max smiled.

"For sure! Mom, where did you last see the creepy garden gnomes?"

She looked around.

"Well, they were in a bag near Heidi and Harley," she said, turning to gesture to the twins. But the twins, who had been happily playing in a pile of upturned potting soil a minute earlier, were gone.

Max looked at Knox.

"I think we have a couple of suspects," he said.

Knox nodded. "Definitely."

They found Heidi and Harley toddling around the backyard. As suspected, the garden gnomes were stacked like blocks on the walkway leading down from the house.

"Case solved," Knox cheered.

"We make an awesome team, bro," Max said. "And I can tell it's going to be an amazing summer!"

About the Author

Kim Roedl was born and raised in Montgomery, Alabama. She is a former newspaper reporter who always hoped to one day break into fiction writing. A Southerner at heart, she enjoys traveling throughout the country with her husband and five children. Kim enjoys reading, shopping, volunteering, and going to community theater performances.

About the Illustrator

Mindy J. B. Whitten, also a born Southerner, is a graduate of Georgia Tech. She currently has one other release, *An Alpaca in My Pocket*. When she is not illustrating, Mindy enjoys her growing family, gardens, and travelling experiences.

Lightning Source UK Ltd.
Milton Keynes UK
UKHW020400110219
337017UK00004B/52/P